WEEKLY READER CHILDREN'S BOOK CLUB presents

Gus Goes To School
story by Jane Thayer
pictures by Joyce Audy dos Santos

(Original title: Gus Was a Real Dumb Ghost)

William Morrow and Company

New York   1982

For Jennifer, with love.

Weekly Reader Books offers several exciting
card and activity programs. For information,
write to WEEKLY READER BOOKS, P.O. Box 16636,
Columbus, Ohio 43216.

This book is a presentation of Weekly Reader Books.
Weekly Reader Books offers book clubs for children
from preschool through high school. For further
information write to: **Weekly Reader Books,**
4343 Equity Drive, Columbus, Ohio 43228.

Published by arrangement with
William Morrow and Company.
Weekly Reader is a trademark of Field Publications.
Printed in the United States of America.

Text copyright © 1982 by Catherine Woolley
Illustrations copyright © 1982 by Joyce Audy dos Santos

Library of Congress Cataloging in Publication Data

Woolley, Catherine.
   Gus was a real dumb ghost.
Summary: A ghost decides to go to school and learn to spell
when a publisher returns his autobiography.
[1. Ghosts—Fiction.   2. School stories]
I. Dos Santos, Joyce Audy, ill.   II. Title.
[PZ7.W882Gw]   [E]   82-2303
ISBN 0-688-01442-9   AACR2
ISBN 0-688-01443-7 (lib. bdg.)

One day Gus the ghost said,
"I've had a lot of adventures.
I think my ghost friends
would like to read about them."
He sat down at his ghostly typewriter
and told Cora the cat and Mouse the mouse
to be quiet.
He began, "I am a gost."

Then he wrote the story of his life
and sent it to a publisher.
The publisher sent it back with a note.
"You have a very good story to tell.
The trouble is that you can't spell."
Gus saw red circles around *gost* and other words.
"What's wrong with g-o-s-t?" he demanded.
Mouse didn't know and didn't care.
Cora said, "Maybe it's spelled g-o-a-s-t.
Or g-o-e-s-t. Or g-o-w-s-t."
Gus looked up those spellings.
"Not in the dictionary.
Well, I am a gost,
and I've got to find out how to spell *gost*!"
"Go to school," Cora advised.

Gus put on his best flowered sheet,
picked up his bang-clank equipment, and trudged off.
He felt a little shy so he asked Mouse to go too.

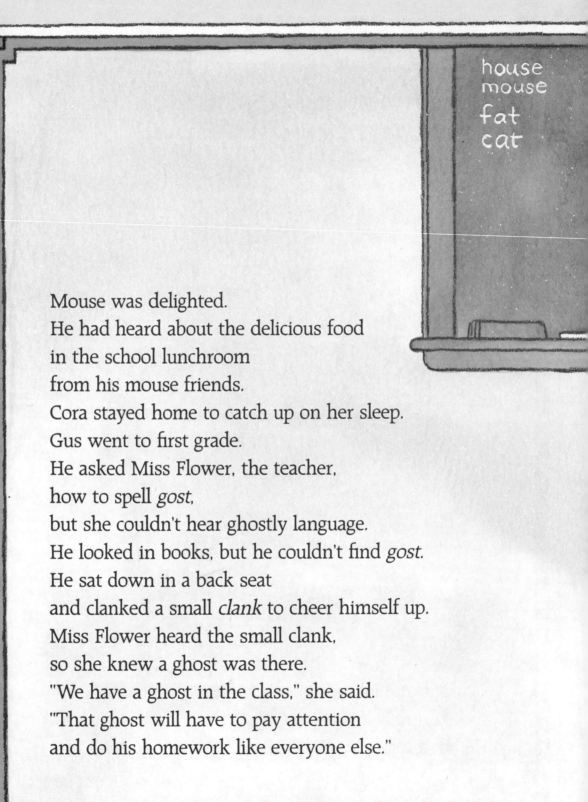

house
mouse
fat
cat

Mouse was delighted.
He had heard about the delicious food
in the school lunchroom
from his mouse friends.
Cora stayed home to catch up on her sleep.
Gus went to first grade.
He asked Miss Flower, the teacher,
how to spell *gost*,
but she couldn't hear ghostly language.
He looked in books, but he couldn't find *gost*.
He sat down in a back seat
and clanked a small *clank* to cheer himself up.
Miss Flower heard the small clank,
so she knew a ghost was there.
"We have a ghost in the class," she said.
"That ghost will have to pay attention
and do his homework like everyone else."

She gave the class words to learn,
such as *if, and,* and *but.*
Gost is the only word I want to spell, Gus thought.
He didn't do his homework,
and he didn't always pay attention.
The only things he liked about school
were recess and lunchtime.
At recess, he played ball with his ghostly ball,
and sometimes he jumped rope.

At lunchtime, he went to see Mouse in the lunchroom.
Mouse had a happy home under the sink
and nine meals a day,
with mashed potato on Monday.

Promotion time came.
Miss Flower said,
"That ghost hasn't done much work,
but maybe he's a slow starter.
I'll promote him."

Gus hoped the second-grade teacher, Mr. Hardy,
wouldn't know he was there and give him work to do,
so he laid his equipment down quietly.
But Mouse came along,
taking his exercise before lunch,
and stubbed his tiny toe on a clanker,
which went *clank*.
Now Mr. Hardy knew about Gus,
and he told him to do his homework.
Gus didn't do his homework.
All he wanted to spell was *gost*.
Why should he bother
with such words as *yesterday* and *today*?
He began to be bored.
He hated school.
He hated Horrible Hardy.
Finally, waiting to find out how *gost* was spelled,
he thought up some pranks to pass the time.

First he coaxed Mouse
into Horrible Hardy's desk drawer.
Horrible opened the drawer and out leaped Mouse,
hungry for his mashed potato.
Everyone screeched until Horrible roared, "Quiet!"
Gus liked that commotion.

Then he took his bang-clank equipment
and marched up and down the halls,
banging like thunder and clanking like crazy.

He took a drink at the water fountain
and squirted water around.

And then, just for fun, he rang the fire alarm.
Clang-g-g-g-g
all over the school.
The children marched out.
Teachers marched out.
Gus marched out.

Fire engines came, sirens screaming.
This was more fun than spelling.
Then the fire chief said,
"False alarm. **Who did this?**"
Miss Flower and Mr. Hardy had heard the bang-clanks
in the hall.
They whispered, "That ghost!"

So, when promotion time came again,
Horrible Hardy said, "That ghost doesn't do his work,
and he is a troublemaker.
He can't go to third grade."
"Oh, no!" Gus groaned.
It had never occurred to him
that he might not be promoted.
He was terribly upset.
People will say ghosts are real dumb, he thought.
My ghost friends will be ashamed of me.
I won't learn to spell *gost*,
and I'll have Horrible again.

Well, I'll haunt him!
He marched around Horrible Hardy,
banging and clanking,
but Horrible was used to noisy children
so he didn't mind noisy ghosts.
"I'll drop out of school," Gus threatened.
But he knew he would never learn to spell *gost* at home.
Finally he calmed down.

He gritted his ghostly teeth, and he thought, Okay.
If I have to do homework, I'll do homework.
One thing I know—
I'm going to be promoted next time.
So he put his bang-clank equipment aside
and settled down to do the homework
Horrible Hardy gave out.
To make sure he'd be promoted next time,
he wrote the new words on the blackboard at night.
After a while, he even wrote a sentence
with his second-grade words:

"What do you know?
That ghost is learning to spell,"
Horrible Hardy said next morning.
Gus was tired of being called "that ghost."
"My name is Gus!" he yelled.
But no one could hear ghostly language.
"How can I tell them?" Gus moaned.

Then suddenly he knew how.
That night he wrote on the blackboard
in large letters:

My name is Gus!

"His name is Gus," the children said next morning.
"Hi, Gus!"
Gus was so delighted that he simply had to bang.
He was getting somewhere!
Then he had another idea.

He hoped that when the children read
what he had written,
they would write the answer.
But they didn't.
They just shouted, "Gus is a ghost!"
His idea hadn't worked.
What a disappointment.
But after a while he thought,
Well, I'm close. What should I do now?
He began to think over all the words
he had learned to spell.
Which ones might help him?
That night he went to the blackboard
and wrote some words.
He erased them.
He wrote more and erased them
and wrote more.

Finally he finished his sentence:

Will some child in this class put down here what Gus is so I can read it?

The next day,
when Mr. Hardy read what Gus had written, he said,
"Who can write *ghost* on the blackboard?"
Gus held his breath.

But the children couldn't spell *ghost* either.
Ghost was a sixth-grade word.
Then Mr. Hardy said,
"We have a ghost in our class,
so we should know how to spell *ghost*."

He went to the blackboard and wrote:

Gus is a ghost.

Gus sat there with his mouth open.
He couldn't believe it.
"That's the way to spell ghost?" he said at last.
Then he grabbed his equipment
and jumped up and down, banging and clanking.

Gus is a ghost.

He rushed to the lunchroom.
"I'm a g-h-o-s-t, Mouse!
Come on home, and we'll tell Cora."
Mouse went right on munching oatmeal cookies.
So Gus ran home
to tell Cora that he was a g-h-o-s-t
and ran back to school again.

That afternoon he wrote on the board:

Today I am a
happy ghost!

Now he loved school.
He even loved Horrible Hardy.
He went on writing all the words
he could think of.
Mr. Hardy said, "Gus can go to third grade."
In third grade,
Gus learned to spell *teacher*,
and he wrote:

I love my teacher.

He clanked his way
to fourth grade
and won a prize for a story called
"Mouse Was a Hungry Monster."

In fifth grade, his favorite word was *Halloween.*

And in sixth grade, he was the first one
to write the word *ghost* on the board.
Now Gus had finished the last grade in the school.

But he didn't want to leave so he wrote on the board:

Dear Teachers and Children,
I have decided to remain
here for forty years and
be the school ghost.
Love from your friendly
ghost,
Gus

The teachers shook their heads.
"Gus should be out in the world
doing a ghost's work.
How can we get him to go?"
Then they said, "Aha! We'll graduate him."
They laid out a graduation gown and hat.
Gus tried them on,
and they were so becoming that he had to wear them.
I'll invite Cora to my graduation, he thought.
But what shall I do all day if I leave school?

Then he remembered
why he had come to school in the first place.
He said to Mouse,
"You may stay and be the school mouse,
and Cora may sleep all day.
I shall be busy rewriting the story of my life."

He walked up the aisle with the graduating class
and nodded politely to Cora and Mouse,
who sat in the front row.